For Lisa, my sister and partner in countless impromptu recitals for "company,"
with love
Bernette Ford

For Iris May Goldsworthy Bennett
love Sam Williams

First American edition published in 2007 by Boxer Books Limited.

Distributed in the United States and Canada by Sterling Publishing Co., Inc.
387 Park Avenue South, New York, NY 10016-8810

First published in Great Britain in 2007 by Boxer Books Limited.
www.boxerbooks.com

Text copyright © 2007 Bernette Ford   Illustrations copyright © 2007 Sam Williams Limited

The rights of Bernette Ford to be identified as the author and Sam Williams as the illustrator
of this work have been asserted by them in accordance with the Copyright, Designs and Patents Act, 1988.

ISBN-13: 978-1-905417-56-8
ISBN-10: 1-905417-56-X

1 3 5 7 9 10 8 6 4 2

Printed in China

Ballet Kitty

Bernette Ford and Sam Williams

Boxer Books

Kitty woke up happy!

Her ears were pink. Her nose was pink.

Even her little toes were pink.

Kitty loved ballet and she loved pink.

And today she was feeling as pretty as

a ballerina—from her head to her toes!

Kitty jumped out of bed

and did a little pirouette.

Then she leaped across her room

to get ready.

Her best friend Pussycat

was coming to play!

Kitty pulled on her pink tights.

She put on her pink leotard.

Then she put on her prettiest tutu.

But something was missing.

"Where are my ballet slippers?"

she said to herself.

Kitty looked in the closet.

She looked in the toy chest.

She looked under the bed,

and all around her room.

But she could not find her ballet slippers.

"MOMMA!"
wailed Kitty.
"I can't find
my ballet slippers."

"Well, wear your
sneakers, then,"
Momma called back.

But Kitty did not want

to wear her ugly old sneakers.

Now Kitty was grumpy.

Her ears were pale. Her nose was pale.

She did not feel happy!

She did not look pretty!

"Where are my ballet slippers?" she mumbled.

"Where could they be?" she grumbled.

Then Kitty heard a knock at the door.

So she pulled on her sneakers.

But a little tear rolled down her face.

"I won't have any fun!" she said

as she went to answer the door.

Pussycat was there,

dressed up like a princess.

And Pussycat looked lovely!

She was wearing her lilac princess gown.

She had on her lilac shoes and her lilac

cape and her little lilac jeweled crown.

Princess Pussycat jumped up and down.

She gave Ballet Kitty a big squeeze.

Together the two friends let out a squeal
and ran to the playroom.

They set up a stage.
They pranced and preened and pretended
to be princesses all morning.

But even princesses can get hungry!

At lunchtime Ballet Kitty set out

her prettiest teacups and plates.

She and Princess Pussycat sat on the floor
while they sipped their juice and nibbled
on little tuna sandwiches.

Then Ballet Kitty kicked off her sneakers.

She showed Princess Pussycat her best pirouettes,

her perfect pliés and her cutest curtsies.

Princess Pussycat tried a pirouette, too.

It wasn't as pretty as Ballet Kitty's.

But that didn't matter.

They put on ballet music and danced

for the rest of the afternoon.

When the day was over and Pussycat went home,

Kitty had a big smile on her face.

Her ears were pink.

Her nose was pink.

And she was feeling happy—

from her head to her little pink toes!

Then she remembered her ballet slippers.

And do you know what?
Ballet Kitty found them—
right there in her room,
under the table.

Just where she had left them

the night before!